Murder:
In Franklin County

Author and Illustration

By: John S. Sylvester SR

Copyrights 2019

First printing. B

ISBN: 978-1-67802-563-2

Dedication

I would like to dedicate this book to Frances Sylvester. She inspired my desire to become a published author. She read Perry Mason mysteries as she raised me.

I know she is proud of this book and my accomplishments as an Author. I remember writing the Pages one by one. She became anxious to read each one.

To my Son John who would have loved this book. He went away to meet his maker. His memory gave me strength to produce each chapter. This book is blessed every day by him. I know Angels are watching over him and blessing this manuscript. I could always call on Angel Boy for advice.

Synopsis

Welcome! You've impressed me with your curiosity! Your about to enter the pages of a book involving Murder. Do you have what it takes? A bone chilling page turner. I wrote this book   to consume your senses. It exhibits sexual behavior.

Our story opens at a Woman's Prison in Indianapolis. The main character is Clara Burns. She is a thoughtless and heartless monster. She has no morals.   She's schizophrenic. A disorder that causes you to behave destructively.

Clara's at the end of an eleven-year bit. She is anxious to be free again.

She dreams of her Freedom. In her heart she knows freedom won't last. She loves to think Murder.

She has a goal. To murder her twin sister. The details are mind blowing. You wouldn't think anyone could plan such detail. It hadn't been written in any Murder mystery.

A shocking plot for a distorted mind. It's unbelievable! The excitement will control your senses. You will begin to shiver as never before! I leave you with one thought!

This is the last warning. Good luck! Turn the page and begin.

Murder:

In Franklin County

Introduction

You are about to enter the dorms of the Indiana Women's prison. It is a massive structure. It is constructed with steel bars.

It could accommodate 599 inmates. It's Indiana's death row for Women. There aren't any women waiting to execution.

These inmates are accused of Felony offenses. They carry one year to life. Due to the longevity of their sentence these Inmates become lonely. Clara has served eleven years. She suffered deeply.

Due to her butch attitude. She did her best dominating other women. She befriended an inmate they developed a relationship.

Clara only agreed to that type of lifestyle for protection purposes. She dug the bitch. She wasn't anyone to write home to Mother.

Her passion for love increased her desire for a partner. It became quite a surprise to feel a strange sensation. Clara would never turn her whole life over to another female.

She was approached by a partner and asked."Why do I feel like This? Thats common in here! Do you think you're the only woman feeling that?"

Most of them won't talk about sex. That's why all these women are chasing each other's!" They had relations.

Clara was hooked. In the heart of a lesbian. Her escapade turned into a full-time desire.

Clara is of great proportion body wise. She weighs 162 pounds but carries it well. She is a full-figured woman. She has an eye-catching sway to her walk. She isn't afraid to shake her shit. A resemblance of a orchestra, hearing an ear catching sound. They check out Clara's bubble butt!

Most of them have approached her. She blows them off. They know about her murderous temper. She is violent. Her partner is jealous of the other inmates. She has taken many of them to fist city.

She was a total crackhead when she was on the street. Satin controlled her. She prostituted to supported her habit. Just one of many things she was involved in. His hold lightened after she was incarcerated.

With a little help from a pipe he will return. She had deep desires for the drug but cleared her mind of it. It's impossible to get her hands on some in her cell block.

In other dorms it is floating around. It would eat up most of the money she had on her books. Clara can't afford to swing it. There is pot floating in the dorm. Not enough to constantly have a buzz.

There is plenty of cash sitting on her books if she really wanted to get high. She avoided the temptation because of losing time.

It isn't worth the risk. It would take just one jealous bitch to run to a guard. Clara's Mother sends money for commissary. Her Mother's name is Sandra Burns.

She sells farm animals at the market for slaughter. In her past her knitting relaxes her. The blankets she knits are exceptional. A friend transports them to her shop in Indianapolis.

The business district is 176 miles due north of Germantown. Close to where Sandra lives. The best time of year for business. Folks from Chicago visit with their families . Indianapolis is the seat of Marion County. The weekends are great. Streets packed with shoppers. The town is all tourists? Sandra lives in Crossville, Tennessee. Just a short jot down I 65 South. She has enjoyed living there. She been there fifty-one years. Everyone living in the area are familiar with the sisters. Not many of them agree on their lifestyle but all to their own. Clara's sister is a twin. Her name is Barbara Cooper.

She was married for three years. Her man ran off chasing after some bimbo to the northeast. The bastard hasn't been seen since. She was thrilled when he left. He went chasing after that two-ton tissuey. She knew he's a philanthropist. He loved handing the whore generous amounts of money.

That was the only way she would give up that ass. She was a genuine gutter girl! Let me tell you she was all ass! She resembled a bag of mango pulp. Stuffed down her drawers.

Her only attractive feature. It was a sick man's fantasy! Barbara knew he was far away. She's enjoying a good life since he left.

Besides for her hair color no one could tell them apart. Barbara had all the boys chasing her when she was a teen. She dated through high school but only with the super good look-in country boys.

She loved when they wore caps or cowboy hats. She loved their blond hair. Many boys in town were blonds. Every year the men appeared to get more handsome as they aged. Clara was in love with the way they looked.

She laid many of them in excitement. She never really had a bag for anyone until she met Charles. He never chased her. She came right to him every time he drove up. She fell in love the first time she saw him.

He flashed wads of money in her face and drove a 1967 GTO! The finest green demon in Crossville. Many of the other teens were jealous. He would let them ride just to calm them down. He would prevent them from vandalizing it. It was funny how Clara and Charles reunited.

He loved her in High-school and tried to date her. She told him to fuck-off on one occasion. He didn't give up on her though. She knew he had a thing for her.

It was one summer night on Rt. 23. There was a car-hop called Henrys. All the class teens hung there. Charles happened to spot her. He saw her on several occasions. He ignored her just to see if she would chase him. One evening she was hanging out at the parking lot. He pulled the green flash into the lot and she melted. The windows were all down and she poked her head inside. With her sexy voice she said "Hello!".

Charles gave her his class ring that night. He remembers Har-path river edge. They became a couple the first time. It stopped other women from seducing him.

Their love was unconditional at that time. She forgot about him after he was incarcerated. Her future with the country boy had ended. It appears that Charles will rekindle the fire that was lost.

The next night Charles visited Henry's restaurant. He planned to catch Clara hanging in the lot. She wasn't there but Leona was. She was an old school friend. It was Clara his heart desired. He asked her where Clara was? She told him at home. She was cooking a cake for her Fathers Birthday.

Leona left the car and phoned her on a pay phone. She told Leona to have Charles go to the park. He did as she requested. He pulled up to the park and seen Clara. She was hot!

She was wrapped in a tight black skirt. Her breasts popped from the front of a cotton top. To finish off the look she wore black hose and shoes. Her outfit was definitely on the slutty side. A street walker would ware that attire.

Looking at her he recalled the rumors around town. They was talk about her slutty behavior. It was the truth!

He couldn't take his eyes off her as she opened the door and sat down. It surprised him that she would dress in that fashion.

They went to the liquor store. They bought beer and wine .Wine was her favorite. Charles drove to the rear of a barn in an alley.

They spent the evening parked there. Together they drank all wine. Charles topped it off with some beers and scored orally.

He is schizophrenic. He was raised by grandparents. He was a troublemaker during his youth. The man served two common addictions. He developed a relationship with demons. He inflicted emotional pain to women.

The grandfather refused him to come back home after his release. Charles was told to keep his distance. His plan was to seduce Clara and move away. Their reputation was tarnished. They rekindled a relationship. Charles was resided at the local Inn.

A few months went by and she moved into the room with him. They spent most of their time getting high and riding his Harley. Clara walked into trouble. He was burglarizing stores at night.

He found a little cabin on Bass lake in Starke County. He was going to invite her to come there with him.

Clara decided she would take Charles up on his offer. The move to Bass lake dld them both a service. She wanted them to have a new start. Charles loved his bad habits. He wanted to commit robberies. He's been doing it alone since they moved to the Lake.

It wasn't too much longer that he had Clara helping him. Just like old times. Charles had a job. It kept him away from home. He drove a truck making deliveries.

On his route he would visit small towns in Indiana and rob store owner of cash. He had gotten away with it so-far. His luck is changed. He asked Clara to take a ride with him. She figured it would be cool. She hopped into the truck. They went out on his route.

The Saga Begins:

No Chapter Numbers

Clara was unaware that Charles packed a gun. They pulled into a small town and stopped at a gas station.

Charles went in and she followed. Clara went into the ladies' room. Charles approached the register.

He told the cashier to open it. He instructed him to hand over the cash. The owner was frightened. While he was collecting the cash, Clara came out of the bathroom.

An Indiana police officer was shopping in the store. Charles was unaware of his presents. Clara spotted him and yelled to warn "Charles. Charles!" She shouted out! As she yelled, the cop pulled his gun. Charles turned around and both guns fired.

What a mistake! The end of their freedom at the end of a gun This officer was hit!

The cop took a bullet to the chest. The sound of the gun fire rang out! Everyone ran in fright.

The officer uniform began to show signs of the open wound. Blood was seeping through his shirt.

He raised his hand and grabbed for his chest in agony. He began to screaming. The feeling of the wound worsened. There was a pause and he fell to the floor. The attendant phoned the police as Charles ran out the door.

Charles dodged the second bullet. He stood in shock knowing he lost his freedom.

He looked for a way out. He began to run. The doorway was blocked with the customers leaving the store in horror.

They wouldn't let him through. He dropped the gun and pushed them. He banged into them. Several of them fell to the floor. He trampled them as he escaped.

The parking lot filled with squads. Police surrounded the station. The two of them were in trouble.

They were handcuffed without further incident. They were taken to the Starke County Police station. The police officer survived the bullet. He was put into an ambulance and transported to the hospital.

Both were charged with robbery and Charles with attempted murder. The two of them were fingerprinted and booked.

There new life took a terrible turn. Into the cells they went. Led down the long hall to the holding cells. The end to her freedom came closer as Clara approached her cell.

They were separated. Charles was detained in a different section with the males. His cube was high security because of his charges.

Clara was pissed. She didn't expect him to do what he did. She was in shock and proclaimed her innocence. The police didn't believe her version.

Her lawyer told her, "It is going to be a long jail stay. At least six months before their first court hearing."

She began yelling down the hallway to the guard, "Sir! Sir!"

"Please let me out! I didn't do anything! Please! I swear! I swear!" She shouted repeatedly.

Another inmate was disturbed by the outbreak and shouted out! "Shut up bitch!" Clara turned and stared at her.The inmate looked back.

She asked, "Who is you? Who is you Bitch!"

Clara responded, "Who the fuck is you bitch? A cop! I need to talk to the guard."

As they continued shouting at each other, another inmate began getting riled.

"Both of you shut the fuck up! Zip your blowhole Ho!" Another inmate shouted.

"Screw you too bitch! Go lay down! All of you shut up and leave me alone! I need this asshole guard to let me talk to the Chief!" Clara explained.

"You think he cares bitch? He not gonna come! You could yell till you"all is red faced. He doesn't give a fuck about your problem. Neither does this cell block! "She shouted in a mean voice. Clara's cellmate reached out. She grabbed a fist of hair from Clara's head.

 "I said shut the hell up Bitch!" She Yelled at Clara.

Clara was pulled away from the bars and thrown to the floor. Clara gave her a few punches to the stomach. It turned into a real cat fight. The guards heard the scuffle in the cell area.

They came running down from their station. Two officers opened the cell door and they each wrestled an inmate on the floor. They managed to separate them.

"Don't resist !" The officer shouted!

"Screw you pig!" The other inmate shouted.

The two of them were separated. They were taken to solitary confinement in the basement. There were five by five cells with a cement floor and a toilet. There was no bunk and no sink for water.

Everything they needed was brought to them. They had to sleep on the cold cement floor. It was a horrible experience for Clara.

It taught her not to get into trouble. Their both spending thirty days in the hole.

There she sat freezing cold on the floor. She was a strong woman. There wasn't even a tear in her eye. The disgrace was horrible, and it angered her. She was regretting the reunion with Charles. He tricked her. The worst part of this whole thing was he didn't tell her his intentions. She was pissed!

The cement was so cold. The corrections officer had no concern. He closed the cell door and walked away. What a sad situation she was pulled into.

There was no going back. She was caged like a wild animal. Wild animals are loved at least. She had no one. Just cold, bare cement walls. How sad it made her.

This episode of incarnation began to torture her emotions. She was split forcefully. Like an ax to a tree stump. Torn apart with no feeling.

She fell asleep. Curled up in a ball on the floor. As a punished child she laid there. Her emotions were gone. She was tough as a bull. She had no idea of what was to come.
Clara fell sleep. She was curled up like a baby. In her sleep she heard a voice calling out. "

"Clara! Clara!" The voice shouted.

It was coming from the cell across the hall. She opened her eyes and look. It was the bitch she quarreled with.

"Hey girl! I am sorry that I caused this. I hope you can forgive me.

Hey baby, I have a joint in my kitty. You could have it! Just a little wait to say I'm sorry. I'm going to take it out. It will cheer you up!. Get up by the bars."She instructed.

 Claire was quite excited! She wanted to get high. She rose and walked over to the bars. The lady turned around in the her cell.

She put her hand down her pants. She took the joint out from her jeans.

She turned and went up to the bars. She got down on her knees. She rolled the joint across floor.

It stopped at the bars surrounding Clara's cell. Right in-front of the cell door.

The girl watched as Clara picked it up.

Clara said. "Thank you girl! This is going to do it. Do you have a lighter?"

 "Yeah ! I do." She threw it to Clara.

Clara sat down on her bunk . She took a few hits

" Let the party begin !"Clara said.

 "I'm going to light this bitch up. You can have the other half." Clara promised.

" Don't be a bog-art! Come on throw it over. Save me a hit". The other inmate said.

Clara took a few hits. She threw it across the hall.

She held the smoke in her lungs as long as possible. If that smoke saturated the hallway it would alert the guard.

"Go ahead and finish it. I've had enough" Clara went to her bed and laid down.

" Oh my God I'm high as hell! This shit is potent bitch!"Clara shouted .

"I told you this shit was good girl. Lay down there and enjoy it."

The other inmate replied.

That's exactly what Clara did. Clara was overwhelmed by the silence. There wasn't any noise down the hall. Suddenly she heard a strange laughing. She began hearing the screams of a lady. She put her hands over her ears. She pushed in harder and harder. She blocked the screens from her ears.

 She opened her eyes. She noticed the girl from across the way. She was standing in her cell . This girl from across the hall. It was a Demon disguised her attacker.

Claire was in a deep dream. It was a horrible dream. Satan was consuming her. The room filled with smoke. Lingering down the hallways. Demon appeared in her cell screaming. It became filled with people. They stood along a wall.

They begun to walk towards Clara. They had death in their eyes. They were the sons of Satan. Demons with black clothing and horns in your four head. One of them stood out from the rest. It was Barbara, her sister.

The voice of Satan filled the room. It was hidden within the smoke. She couldn't see anyone talking.

"I'm Satan Clara. I've consumed your mind and body with death. I'm going to take your soul to hell! I will be with you when you wake up. We have become one. You will be under my control. Do you see Barbara?" Satin asked.

"Yes! " Clara responded.

"Kill her! Kill her!"Satan yelled.

His hands raised to the ceiling. A knife was clinched in his fist. He swooped down. He gave it to Clara. Suddenly, Barbara lifted up a pair of scissors towards Clara.

Satan told Barbara,"Take those scissors and kill your sister. Let's see who's going to win!

The both of them were stabbing each other. Cutting into their flesh. Without warning Satan disappeared. She watched as Barbara also vanished. Barbara wasn't seen again.

The guard heard the commotion. He ran to her cell. He took the keys and open the door. He noticed Clara was sleeping yet screaming. The girl across the hall was clinched against the bars.

She was frightened for Clara. Clara was totally consumed with visions of Demons. The guard went down and shook her. He woke her. He put her head in his arms.

He said," Clara you're dreaming wake up. Wake up! Clara opened her eyes." He said.

"Thank you! I'm scared to death. It was horrible! Satan was laughing . Satan told me to take the knife he had. It's time to kill my sister! Take them! Over and over Satan repeated the command. Then everyone disappeared." She explained.

The guard looked in amazement. He turned to Clara and said, "I here don't worry. You were dreaming. I'm right down the hall if you need me.

Lay down and try to go to sleep. Everything is fine. Relax."

He stood up and turned. He walked out of the cell. He locked the cell door behind him. He walked down the hallway.

Claire turned over and closed her eyes. It didn't take long for her to fall asleep.

Clara slept all night. She was shaking when she woke . The girl across the hall was awake.

"Girl that was a real bad dream I had last night. That shit really kicked my ass." Clara shouted.

The other inmate replied," Me too babe I was gone. I heard you screaming." She told Clara.

"By the way. You were here too. In my cell girl! You were a Demon! A Demon with your body! It was the weirdest dream I ever had. I don't know how I made it through. Things don't look good for me.

The future is very bleak. She had to be strong. A weak person in her position won't make it out. They learn to appreciate the freedom life once offered. It was important she learned to show no emotion. This is best for any inmate at the beginning of their bit. It will make them strong in the eyes of others.

They will tempt you. You need to exhibit your strength. They pick at you. Then throw insults to break you. They see how much shit you will stand for.

To begin a sentence is pure hell. To do the time is even worse. It doesn't get any better. It only gets worse each day. You must be tough and hold your own. No-one will come to your aid. You're in there alone and you do your time alone. No one cares.

Clara became adjusted to her stay. She knew the big house was going to be overwhelming for her. The trial was a week away. She was preparing a defense for her case. She didn't have much of one. All because of stupid Charles.

Day by day she withstood the insults and sadness from the others. She was thankful to be out of her five by five cell. She could have a blanket and a shower in the cell block. She would have to be pushed before she would explode again. She needs to exercise strong control. Every moment was hell.

The days became easier. She had to adjust.In the morning she would face the Judge. It made her quite nervous but comforting to face it. The day went by quickly and it was dawn. She went to bed to be fresh for the morning.

The sun rose early, and the transport team came for her. She was let out of the call and walked up the hall. The court building was across the street. In the distance she spotted Charles being transported. He didn't see her as the door to the court closed behind him.

It was the first she began to cry. She knew it was over. Her relationship had come to an end. She felt alone and unwanted. She became paranoid as the door closed behind her.

The officer paid no attention to her. They were cold like as if they were walking a dog. No emotions on their faces. Just a cold stone look. Once inside they pointed the way. Not one word of instruction did they speak.

They pulled at her arms. She was led into the courtroom. Each inmate was in a line against the wall. They were lined up like circus clowns waiting to perform. They stood insulted like a line of buffoons. People in the room laughed at them.

There one-color orange suits should be replaced with a polka dotted uniform. They were not allowed to sit. They were handcuffed to one another like a chain gang.

They became tired as they stood in line. They began sloping to the floor as their knees became weak. There were no tricks to be played in this arena. This was far from entertaining.

The room was open and cold. The Judge seat wasn't filled. They were waiting to hear their faith. It was a frightening experience for Clara and the others. They didn't mutter a word as they stood in silence.

The seats started to fill with onlookers and witnesses. People kept coming into the room.The guard stopped them.

He began shouting across the court. "Sorry but everyone that isn't seated must wait outside. Please exit and close the door.

Everyone in this court please turn off your phones. No talking! Everyone stand please! Judge Mathew is about to enter! Court is in session."

Silence filled the room as the Judge entered and sat down.

Her day in court went quickly. She was sentence to eleven years. Shipped off to the Women's Detention Center in Indianapolis, Indiana.

She was transported to a bus waiting outside. It was mid fall and the air was cold. She had no jacket. They marched in line to the door of the bus. They were unchained as they approached the door. Each inmate took a seat and looked through the windows. Outside the metal walls of the bus was freedom.

A silence filled the bus as the doors began to close. The driver started the engine. They began their trip to the prison wall. It was going to be the beginning of a different life for each of these inmates. Clara was loosing her breath. Her heartbeat quickened. It was a one-hour ride to the prison. The bus approached the entrance.

The bus pulled through the gate and rolled to a stop. The felling of freedom really became a memory. She had a clear view of the courtyard ahead. What a frightening sight for all of them. The inmates peered through the windows. The new inmates stood in front of them.

The sight of their new surroundings. A cement wall imprisoned everything. Even the cell blocks were inside a ten-foot brick wall. There was no escaping now. She knew the bus just rolled away with her future.

It was scary and without love. The door opened. Her stomach dropped. She knew it was her first walk into hell. She rose from her seat and moved towards the door. She was instructed to walk off the bus.

"Keep your mouth shut." The guard shouted.

She followed the Guard instructions. Shaking at every step forward.

All the inmates followed her. She was first in line. At the last step a Guard pointed at her. "You! Move over here! And the rest of you follow! Now! Move it!" He shouted

They marched in a single line as his instructions. "Drop those bags to the ground! Answer as your name is called. No talking and look forward."

Clara was the ninth person called and she replied as requested. "Here!" She yelled!

"Those names I called are to move in a separate line. The next group! Form a second line." The guard instructed.

Clara was in the first line. They were going into the dangerous criminal side of the prison. These inmates are locked up twenty-four hours a day. There is no movement. Everything they need is brought to them.

They live in open dorms with fifty beds per section. They'll have a toothbrush, a change of clothes and shower shoes in their possession. That was it.

Everything else was taken away and put into the property room. They would get it back upon their release. They could choose to have it sent to a relative if preferred.

They were led inside the main hall and to the clothes room.

"One at a time walking up to the window and get your uniform!"

The guard instructed.

"State your size! Small, medium, and extra- large. Tell the clerk what you need!" Another guard shouted!

Each inmate moved in line as they collected their uniforms. They were moved into the shower room. They were told to remove their clothes.

They stood in line naked as each name was called. That person had to walk up in front of the guard. One by one they spread their ass cheeks. It was a cavity check for contraband.

"If you are caught with anything in a cavity you will be charged with another Felony! Understood! If there is anything this is your chance to get rid of it! Take it out in front of the guard. "Hand it to the Officer." The correctional officer stated.

After the inspection they were led into a shower room. They were sprayed down with an insecticide. The prisoner's bodies were all cleaned of body lice.

The last stop before they went to the dorm was the doctor. Each inmate received different shots depending upon their examination. Each inmate visited the doctor. They sat in line for about a half hour per inmate. This was to assure the inmates their health was safe.

'Off to the dorm! Finally!' Clara told the inmate behind her.

"Shut up Bitch! Just keep your ass moving." Another Inmate shouted.

Then another shouted, "Screw you! Who is you? Who is you?"

"I'm your worst nightmare ho! I'm going to beat your ass the moment the guard leaves us alone. Got that lady!" She shouted

The line moved forward as the guard shouted,

"You two inmates that want to fight step to the rear of the line. You are in big trouble. This will be your first write -up." He said to the inmates.

The ladies did as he instructed, and another guard took them away to solitaire.

Clara had served her eleven years. She had a rough time but survived. She just returned from chow. It was evening and dinner was complete. She was thinking about her release in the morning.

She decided to stay in her bed area. That would keep her arms away from the other inmates. It was best she didn't get into a scuffle. They all knew she was going home. Tension tightens when a person is getting out.

"Shit! I need to call Evelyn! I wonder how close she is to the front gate!" She thought to herself. She sat up and looked towards the phones. The line wasn't so long. She rose and stood in line.

It didn't take long. She made it to the phone. She dial Evelyn's number and heard her voice."Hello!"

"Evelyn is that you? "Clara asked?

"Yeah! It's me bitch!I'm on my way. I'll see you at eight in the morning. I'll be out at the gate". Evelyn said.

"I hope you brought a joint and some beers. Party! party!party! Did you get a room in town yet? "She asked.

"No not yet."Evelyn replied.

"OK! See you in the morning. I have to get off the phone. There are people waiting."Clara hung up the phone

As she was walking away she stopped by another inmate.

"Come on girl let's go in the john and smoke a J. It's your last night here.I'm going to miss you. Clara followed her into the women's bathroom and they lit up. They both hugged.

Clara said "I have to get back to my bunk. I still need to pack my gear."

She turned and walked out of the John. She reached her bed area and set down. She started rumbling through her things to see what she was going to keep. She planned on discarding some belongings. She was so high she couldn't finish the task. She laid down and fell asleep till morning.

Morning came fast. It was 8 AM and she awoke. The guard was walking towards her.

"I thought you'd be up waiting for me to come get you "He said..

"This is the first time during my bit I'm happy to see you!"Clara stated.

She jumped out of bed. She went to the ladies room washed her face and combed her hair. She forgot her toothbrush but she said to hell with it. She just wanted to get out of there.

She walked back to her bed area with a smile. She was going to depart from the penitentiary. The guard told her to follow him.

He led her to the gate. She stepped through and turned around. She looked at him and just smiled.

"Don't come back here now "He said to her.

A voice in the distance yelled, "I'm here Clara! I'm here!?

Clara turned and seen Evelyn waiting for her. She ran up to her. They gave each other a hug.

Evelyn was so happy to see her. After hugging they both jumped in the car and drove off. They didn't drive too far and Evelyn pulled into a roadside in. It wasn't the best place but it was cheep.

Evelyn had a joint and some beer in the trunk. She stop and parked.They got out. Evelyn went to the back of the car and pop the trunk.

"I got some beers here! Bitch energy."She said.

"Cool!"Clara exclaimed.Let's go inside and get high! I waited a long day for this night. Can't wait to get messed up".

Evelyn notice a club down the street.

"Look! Clara! Truckers love paying for ladies drinks." Evelyn said.

"Where is the bar."Clara asked.

"It's there!"Evelyn replied. Let's get fucked up! Get changed and we'll go over there."

"Come on girl lite that joint." Clara said. Evelyn did as Clara asked. They lit the joint and smoked it. Clara got blasted.

Evelyn was looking out the window to the bar.

"Change your clothes bitch. Let's get over there. Look! Hot men hanging tough." Evelyn commented.

The two of them change their clothes and out the door they went. They walked up to the door of the bar and a gentleman opened it for them. They walked inside and sat at the bar. The place was a meat market. There were all sorts of men. Most of them were truck drivers.

They ordered a few drinks. A man behind them said to the bartender, "I'll take care of that."

The ladies turned and thanked him. Clara noticed the hunk leaning against the wall. He was drunk. She thought she would go talk to him. She left Evelyn at the bar and walked over and said. "Hello."

He turned in amazement. "What's up girl." He said.

Clara looked at him with a smile. She had a glare and an urge for him. She noticed his muscular body. He looked strong. His arms were all muscle. She admired his handsome face. He had blonde hair,5'10" tall. He was what she dreamed of for 11 years. "Oh,! My God!" She said. "This is a hot man!"

She sat and talked to the man for about 20 minutes. He paid for a few drinks a few smiles. He asked her to dance. She admired him. They got up and went to the dance floor.

In the meantime Evelyn picked up this other trucker. They had a few drinks and talked for a while. He told her he was from Covington Kentucky.

He was cute and she admired him. She decided to do him. She looked down at his man area. He was hung. She wanted him. He turned to her and asked," Want to go to the truck?"

She didn't want to be easy.

"Let's sit for awhile. I want too think about this."She answered. She called Clara's phone. Clara stopped dancing to answer it.

"What's up bitch? Did you like what you found? I knew you were going to call and tell me to come over there. Am I right?" Clara said.

"You got it! This guys got a pocket full of cash. I'm going to get him in the truck and get his pants off. Wow!

This is going to be good. I'll get him in the sleeper. Open the door. Grab his drawers. Take what's in his pockets and throw them back on the floor. Quietly close the door behind you." Evelyn explained.

Clara did as she was instructed. When she got the money she ran quickly back to the room. She went in and lock the door.

She began peering out the window to make sure Evelyn got out. Both of them climbed out of the truck. Clara beginning to get nervous. He kissed her and she walked away.

She went back to the bar as he got in the truck and drove away. She waited a bit then went back to the room.

We did it girl. How much did you get. A bunch baby. This will get us all the way back to Tennessee and another room.

They were surprise. He was carrying $600 in his pocket. They put the roll in the drawer. Both of them bedded down. It was a long ride he Franklin Tenn.

Clara got out of bed. She used to John and freshened up. She put her clothes on. She looked at Evelyn Lying on the bed. She decided to get her up. She kicked the bed and said,"Come on let's go".

Evelyn rose and stretched. She was still a little tired from the night before. Evelyn got up and use the John. She washed and brushed her teeth. She came back in the room and got dressed.

When she went for her earrings they were gone."Where the hell are my earrings? Evelyn said. Shit! I dropped them in the truck. I had them when I went in." She said.

"The trucker has to have them. Let's get some breakfast. Get the car. We're going to drive to Covington Kentucky. We're going to find that motherfucker. If he doesn't give me those diamonds back I'm gonna blow his head off. I might just do it anyhow for the trouble."Clara responded.

They did exactly as planned. They drove the Covington Kentucky. It took them four hours from where they were. They pulled in the drive across the street.

They noticed his truck. He's sleeping in the back or he isn't there. They waited. He appeared. He went home for something.

 He got out of his car and went to the trunk. Evelyn pull the car around next to his. Clara jumped out of the car with a gun in her hand. Get the fucking diamonds cock sucker!" She said.

Don't shoot he replied. I have them up in the truck. Get up there and get the fuckers. She held the gun on him.

He jumped up in the truck and grab them. He came back out. "Get in the backseat of car." She instructed.

He did as she asked. Clara followed him and sit down next to him. Evelyn hit the gas and he drove off. I'm driving to Gatlinburg.

During the ride to Gatlinburg they pulled into a wooded area. Evelyn stop the car and turned it off. She turned and said,"Get out." He did and Clara followed him.

The three of them walked into the wooded area. They walked past the brush in the juniper plants. The thicket was getting deep in the trees and was getting larger.They were deep in the woods. Evelyn grabbed the gun from Clara and shot him in the back. He displayed pain as he fell to the ground.

They checked his pants for more money and took his wallet. They dragged him into a cave.Then covered him with some leaves and brush. Then they left. The two of them ran back to the car, jumped in and drove away. They had no concern for him.

"Look at me I'm all full of blood". Evelyn stated.

Just drive a little bit down the road. There is a pond you could wash. They followed the curve around to the pound. Evelyn stopped the car and turned the engine off.

They walked through the path. The path curved around down to the pond. They reached the pond. Evelyn removed her clothing. She walked to the edge of the water.

"Go ahead! Get in the water! Clara told her. Get that shit off of you.Lets get the hell out of here."Clara said.

Evelyn did as Clara instructed. She walked deeper into the water.There was a sludge under her feet. She began to sink.

"Help! I'm sinking. Satin interrupted."

Taking over Clara's senses. He stoned her emotions. She had no feelings for Evelyn. As she sank into the water. She disappear. Screaming yelling for her to help. Clara ignored her. She did as Satan instructed.

Clara was ruthless. She didn't even shed a tear for her girlfriend. She ran to the car. She threw Evelyn's clothes in the trunk. Then drove back to the cave. She went back in. She carried Evelyn's clothing.

She laid the clothes by the truckers body. She ran out. It was starting to get dark. She was getting tired. That didn't stop her from driving. She was determined to drive home.

Clara was on going I 40 eastbound. Her eyes were getting heavy. She was beginning to get tired. There was a sign on the side of the road.It advertised a bar called "The Cheer Poppers." Just 15 miles ahead.

Clara was familiar with the bar. She went there many times while dating Charles. It a roadside dive converted into a bar. She remembered a musty smell inside.

She didn't care what It smelled like. She pulled off the highway an stopped at the stop sign. She turned and there was Poppers. She pulled into the parking lot and parked. As she was getting out she noticed a familiar face.

She had to look twice at him. She recognized him.

"That's the fucker! I was going with before Charles. I caught that bastard cheating on me. Two timing asshole with a bimbo."

She reached down in the consul and grabbed a switchblade. It was tucked away in the consul. She hit the lock on the door and closed it. It was only a short jot to the front door.

She pulled on the handle and it opened. The music was blasting as usual in a bar. There was a handful of people drinking. Several couples were dancing on the floor. Just as many people standing around. The back of the bar had a pool table. The cue sticks were in a stand mounted on the wall.

Dustin was the man's name that walked in the bar ahead of her. She looked around at a few men. None of them look like him. She thought she was mistaken. She just figured she was wrong. She walked over to the bar and ordered a drink.

No one in the bar recognized her. There were more ladies up at the bar than men. She wasn't there to pick up anything so it didn't bother her.

She got her drink and she stood at the end of the bar.

She was enjoying her drink when she spotted him. He was leaning against the wall by the pool table. He spotted her.

He began shouting. "Clara ,Clara ,over here!"

He wasn't aware that she spotted him earlier. Now is my chance. I will get my revenge. I already killed twice tonight. What the hell I'm going for it. The fucker made a big mistake with me. Then he goes and dates my sister. That's another reason why.I hate that broad.

She was getting very upset thinking about the situation. The man's name was Dustin. He was a dark haired man with a good built.

She remembered his name shortly after he yelled for her.. He was making it through the crowd over to. He joined her at the bar

Clara noticed the room starting to fill with a strange fog.She wasn't paying attention. Screw Dustin and the small talk. She was more worried about the fog. It was Satan! He was darkening the room. Is was about to happen as before. Guess who? Satan!

She became frightened. Satan scared her to death. She looked around the room. Dustin turned and told Clara to turn around. There's a spirit behind you. I have never seen a spirit like that before. Satan! Dustin screamed! The room became filled with fog.

Satan put Clara's hand into her purse. She was totally under his control. He wrapped her hand tightly around the handle of the blade. He lifted her hand. She stabbed him right into the side of his neck. She watched his blood run his down shirt.

He was screaming in agony. Everyone started running out of the bar. There was a lot of turmoil and people screaming. The men were guiding the women out of the front door. No one noticed Dustin as he fell to the floor. He hit it hard. With a loud thump.

There was too much commotion. Clara took her hand off the knife. Satan covered her with thick smoke. She became almost invisible. No one saw her run out the door.

He got her to the car. The keys were already in the ignition. The car was running. She put the car in drive and drove off. There were police sirens sounding in the distance. Police cars coming from every direction. She hit the expressway ramp and headed west to Franklin. Satan disappeared.

Clara was scared to death. Satin appeared again. She turned the radio on real loud. She stomped on the gas and drove quickly down the road. She passed cars at a high rate of speed. She was running and didn't care.

Running from Satan, from a murder, running from life with no place to go. Except for the motel room. She was freaking out. It was another two hours to Franklin. She was exhausted by the time she got off the ramp. She was happy to see the Motel in the distance

She couldn't handle all the blood on her. She needed to wash it off. Her hand and arm were soaked in it.

She arrived at the Inn, She went into the room.she took off her clothes and showered. The car had to disappear. Junkers pickup these cars all the time. She didn't want any money for it. She just wanted it gone!

She looked up a junkyard in the phone book. She called. They wanted a title. There wasn't one that would take it. She searched and persistence paid off.

She located one that would take it. No title needed. She instructed them to come and pick up the car. She knew it would be the first thing cops would look for.

One hour later the tow truck arrived. He backed up to the car and hooked it up. Put the chains on and drove away.

Clara called the car rental agency They came and picked her up. She sign for the car and drove back to the room. She went inside and fell fast asleep.

The next morning Clara Rose and got dressed. She was going to visit her mother in Crossville. She grabbed her purse and put on a sweater. She got in the car and drove away.

She drove down I 65 an hour and a half to Crossville. She knew where her mother lived. She had no problem finding the house. She got out of the car and walked up to the door. She knocked at the door and waited.

 A woman appeared at the door. It was her Mother.

"Clara can't believe your out! It's so nice to see you! Come on in. When did you get out?" She asked.

"I've been out a few days I'm staying up in Franklin. I figured I would drive down here today. I wanted to talk to you about my sister. I heard she received Uncles inheritance. That's real good news mother. Did he leave me anything." She asked.

"Yes,Clara.She has a trust account for you,$50,000. Tomorrow,I'll call her and let her know you're back. I'll get the information and help you claim your money. It's at some bank here in Crossville." She said.

"That's cool Mom! Oh! That's my number save it. Her mother walked into the other room. She came back with a pen and paper. She wrote it down" She said.

"Are you still fighting with your sister? I wrote to Charles in Michigan City. I didn't like what he wrote back. He told me you had planned to murder your sister. I hope that's not true??"

"You know how I feel about her Mother. I hate her. If I get my hands around her neck. I'm gonna choke the life out of her. That bitch better stay far away from me. In time I'll carry out my plan. It sounds horrible. That's the way it is." She stated.

"How could you sit here and tell your Mother you're planning to murder your sister. I didn't find that very amusing. Don't say anymore. I just can't believe that this is going on." She responded.

Mom. I'm going to do what I have to do. I'm a big girl. Keep your nose out of it. Act like you don't know anything about it. Clara stayed there for a few more hours. They had a pleasant conversation and some dinner. Then She left.

Clara started to drive back to the motel. She said to herself. As long as I'm in Crossville I'm gonna look for Barbara's house.

She drove south on the expressway. She got off at the Crossing exit and went to the house in division. She knew the house was somewhere in the development. She drove around for a little bit.

"There it is!"Clara said in her mind. "That's a Beautiful house. It will be mine once I plug her."

Clara sat in the car. She parked the front. She noticed Barbara come out the front door. She had retrieved the newspaper. While she was sitting a cop car pulled up. It parked in front.

Clara scooted down in the front seat not to be seen. He got out of the car and walked to the door. She looked up. She had a clear view of him. She started the car and drove off.

Claire was going north on I 65 out of Town. It would only take a few hours to make it back to the motel. While she was driving it started to drizzle. She proceeded north and the rain pounding the window. Harder and harder. She could hear the hail hitting the roof in the trunk of the car.

Without warning Satan appeared. She looked at him and screamed. He was on fire. His eyes were red. He had horns on his head. He freaked her out. She never saw him in that fashion. She couldn't see out the windshield. She pulled off to the side of the road. She stops the car and Satan begin to speak.

"Scared? Are you? I'm gonna continue to scare you Clara! You are going to finish off your sister! I've planted this in your mind."He said.

Clara was frightened. She just wanted to get away from him. She opened the car door and ran into the woods. He chased after her. She ran as hard as she could but he was still behind her. She turned to look for him. She couldn't see him. Was he still there? There was a tree stump in the brush. She tripped over it and fell forward.

She scraped her knees and arms. She turned around and look up. Satan was over her. He appeared in a cloud of smoke.

He said."I'll kill you too! Soon," He disappeared quickly.

Clara got up and ran to the car. She ran as fast as possible. She had tears in her eyes. She was trembling. His look was scary. He had a murderous demeanor. One of a madman.

She made it to the car. She opened the door, set down. She started it and drove off. As she was driving she trembled. It wouldn't stop causing her to sway.

She began talking to herself. She told herself she was done with Franklin. She would be leaving Franklin first thing in the morning. Her mind told her the place was haunted. The Franklin Inn is bad for me. She was going back to Indianapolis. She would stay there till Charles got out of the penitentiary.

Clara wasn't in the clear yet. The police are beginning to look for her. They were at Barbara's house talking to her. While they were there Barbara called her mother.

Her mother drove over to Barbara. She wanted to talk to the officer. She was doing this for Clara. When she arrived at Barbara's she greeted her.

Come in Mother. She stepped into the front room and noticed the tall dark officer. He was African-American and was built well. She walked towards him and put her hand out.

"Hello I'm Sandra Burns."She said.

He responded by saying"Hello Mam!" Barbara begin speaking. Mother!This gentleman is here looking for Clara. He just got through telling me a story. It was about a man that disappeared from Indianapolis. He knows that Clara and Evelyn drove down here. He's looking to talk to them.

"What was your name Officer?" She asked.

"Officer Fuller Mam." He replied.

"Officer I have no idea where Clara is. I haven't heard from her. Did she stop here ? Is that how you found this house? Well Barbara? She questioned Her."

"No Mother!" She replied.

They spoke for another hour. Officer Fuller interrogated them.

His questions were answered and he was satisfied. They didn't know where she was. Both of them assured the officer if they heard from her they will call him.

Officer Fuller was pleased with the information he received. He left the residence. Then walked to his car sat down and drove off.

Clara made it back to the motel. She was exhausted from the drama she experienced. It was the scariest thing that ever happened to her in life. She couldn't wait to get back in the room. She never wanted that to happen again. Especially not in the car while she was driving.

She gather her things together. She put them by the suitcase. She couldn't pack them. She needed clothes for Morning.

She planned an early departure. She pulled down the covers and got into the bed. She laid there thinking of the horrible experience she had.

It frightened her. He wanted to kill her. No one threatens like that. It was serious. While she was thinking she fell asleep.

The sun rose early and Clara was asleep. She was unaware there were cops surrounding the motel. They were on the hill. There were snipers with guns surrounding her room. She was done. There was no place for her to run.

There was a knock at the door. Clara woke up. "Who's there?" Clara said.

"Tennessee state police! Open the door!"

The Officer shouted.

He pounded fiercely at the door.

Clara refused to open it. She put on her clothes then reached for her gun. She crouched down. She used a small table for cover.

"I'm not coming out!" She shouted.

She knocked out a pane of glass. By using the handle of the gun. She began to fire at the officers. They stormed the door. It gave away from the frame.

A police dog entered. Clara panicked when she seen the dog. The dog jumped at her and started biting at her leg. Claire was quite frightened. She just laid there . She was frozen. She couldn't move. The dog scared her immensely.

The officers came in showing their guns. "Don't move! Put your hands behind your back!" They demanded.

She did as they instructed. Two officers cuffed her. The third grab the gun and disarmed it. She walked out to the squad car and was put in the back seat.

The officers drove the cruiser to the police station. They took her into the lock up. There she sat until her court date. She was charged with Dustin's murder at the bar. They had several witnesses that identified her. They also had the license plate number of the car.The car was impounded.

Clara sat in a 5 x 5 cell staring at the walls. She began talking to herself. "Look where you've put me you bastard! You've ruined my freedom. You caused me to take those lives. Leave me alone! Leave me alone! Satan!

I want to be free of you! Please! She put her head down by her legs and started crying. What have I done? What?"She said repeatedly.

An officer happened to be walking past her cell. He noticed her crying and in distress. He grabbed the bars and said,

"Clara are you OK? Is there anything I can get for you?"

Clara turned to him and said,

"Can you tell me how they got to the motel.

This is the story I heard from the officers. They found your car. The Officer called for backup. Six other squads came to the scene. A squat team surrounded the motel. They walked up the hill carrying shotguns.

The swat team broke the door down. Once they let the dog in the situation was all over. You know the rest.

That morning officer Fuller Clara's mother. He informed her Clara was in custody for murder. He asked her to go to the Motel. He informed her that Clara's things needed to be picked up an the car had been impounded.

Sandra called Barbara and told her of Clara's situation. Barbara was so happy she didn't get too worked up. She felt safer because she knew Clara's plan.

Barbara sat down and wrote Charles a letter at The prison in Indiana. She told him about Clara. She wouldn't be able to come and get him. Enclosed in the envelope she sent a bus ticket to Franklin.

She invited him to stay at her house. She told him she has a car and plenty of money. He had to get a job though. She was looking forward to seeing him. I will pick you up at the bus station. He was instructed to call her when he arrived.

Barbara called Sandra and asked her to come to the house. She wanted to discuss Claire's arrest. She called Fuller. She asked him to come to the house. Two days later,

they gathered in her living room.

Barbara started the conversation.

She turned to Fuller and said'" What is going on with Clara? Who was the man she murdered? Did she know him? "

"His name is Dustin Conners. They were in a bar just 20 miles east of Franklin on I 40. She went in there to have a drink evidently. She saw him. According to witnesses.

She invited him to the bar. He was standing by the pool tables. The witnesses claimed the room filled up with a strange fog.

Clara was being controlled by Satan. He stood behind her! Took her hand and pushed it in her purse. She grabbed a knife that was inside. He totally controlled her.

He lifted her arm and she stabbed Dustin on the right side of his neck. Witnesses stated. Everyone froze in place.

They ran in different directions. They didn't see much after that. But they did notice her get into a red compact. She drove away.

When the officer's busted into the hotel. They went into the bathroom. They found blood on her clothes. Blood on the sink and drops on the floor. This was the proof they needed. A cold blooded Murderer!. Clara! She went to the sink to wash off the blood. Then changed her clothes. Her charge is first-degree murder. Were holding her in Franklin County Jail.

She will be arranged in about a month. Her court dates on the 27th. She does need a lawyer. If you can't afford one she could hire a state attorney. I really don't recommend it. This girl is in big trouble.

We're dealing with the disappearance of a trucker. Clara and her girlfriend picked up in Indianapolis. Plus the disappearance of Evelyn. This girl has been busy! We believe three murders were committed by Clara. I intend to prove it." Fuller concluded.

"I know that Dustin! Officer Fuller! I dated him after Clara broke up with him. That was years ago. She caught him cheating on her. They had a little brawl. She was very hurt and gave him his ringback. They were engaged for two years."Barbara said.

"I knew something was going to happen to him. She told me if she ever ran into she would kill him. She must have run into him. That was all she needed.

 She a schizophrenic. She's mentally Ill. She goes into a rage in a second." Barbara told Fuller.

Well! this is quite an unfortunate incident. I didn't want to come and bring you bad news. This is my job though. Let me know if I can be of any assistance.

Fuller open the door and left. He walked to the car . He drove away quickly. Barbara turned and faced her Mother."Get the money from the bank. Bail her out. $50,000 dollars.

"She could use it for her defense. We could bond her out. "Barbara said.

"Go get her money mother. I don't recommend putting it up for her bond. There will be more trouble. But if that's what you want to do. I can't stop you." Barbara told her.

"She has the right to use the money. The way she wants. Your uncle left it to her. Go to the bank and get it and open an account. She will decide what to do."Barbara stated.

"Keep Clara away from me Mother." She responded.

"I have to! We'll figure it out. Come on Barbara walk me to the door." Sandra asked.

"Be careful going home. Don't let this bother you. I know you're going to be thinking about it all night. She has it coming. She's a bitch! Barbara said. Sandra walked out the door and Barbara close it.

The next morning Barbara Rose from bed. She got dressed and she went to the bank. She signed the papers for the trust to be released. She opened an account for Clara and deposited the money. Once that was done, Barbara went to jail. When she arrived at the desk she asked Sargent to see Clara.

"She was not allow any visitors." The Officer said.

"I have bond money for her. " Barbara responded.

There is no bond at this time!. Her bond hearing next Wednesday." The Officer said.

She was disappointed. She walked back out to the car. She's never been involved in Police activities. There was nothing else for her to do. Since

Clara wasn't allowed any visitors. Barbara decided to write her a letter.

She went home and begin writing. Clara I hope this letter finds you well. There was an officer at your sisters house his name is Fuller. He told us what you did or what they're accusing you of. I can't believe that you would do that. Barbara said she knows that Dustin guy.

I know it's hard to tell you not to worry. But I am here to help you. Your sister gave me the passcode for the trust account. I went to the bank and got the money out and put it in another account. Barbara said she knew that Dustin guy. There's $50,000 for your hearing on the

27th. I will be in the court. Don't worry everything's gonna be

Clara's court hearing came and went. She was able to bond out. The bond was $30,000 in cash. Her mother brought it to the courthouse and paid the bond. She had no other place to go. She didn't have a car. Her mother took her to her house. Claire wasn't too happy to stay there. She thought it would be best.

The stay with her mothers was stressful . She didn't like having a babysitter. Her mother really tighten her freedom an drove her everywhere she had to go. She drove to for all her court hearings. They went together to visit the attorney.

At different times they went out to eat. Clara wasn't left too far from site of her Mother.

Barbara didn't tell Clara that Charles was on the way to Franklin. He called her that morning and told her he was getting on the 9 AM bus. He got out at 8 AM that morning. It was a four hour ride to Crossville. She was going to pick him up at two thirty. She was meeting him at the Bus stop.

Barbara was thrilled that Charles was going to stay with her. Barbara didn't know that Charles loved Clara. She didn't know him and Clara are plotting against her. She felt like Charles was coming there to love her. She knew this would be a betrayal to her sister. Barbara was thrilled that Charles was going to live with her.

Let's shift our thoughts on Charles. Since he's going to Barbara when he gets out. Let's find out what he's doing. How is he passing his time?

It's chow time. The men are all lined up to receive their meal. They go to chow in shifts. Charles walks behind his friends. They walk up to the service counter.Then their given portions of food.

The lines keep moving. Each selection is distributed per inmate. They are only allowed 15 minutes to eat and drink. It's done swift. There is no time for chat. One by one they following the line to the door. They prepare to be escorted back to the dorm.

"Last call for movement! Dorm two line up we are ready for a headcount. Please face me and keep your traps shut! Do you understand!" The guard shouted.

After completing the headcount the guard dismissed them. The men walk forward to the dorm. Once they were inside the door closed behind them. The dorm held 200 bunks.They were allowed a nightstand with a property box. This was all they were allowed. The beds were in rows of 50.

It was 11 AM in the morning. Charles was waiting for the mail. Walked up to the guard station. The guard left his post and went to the door. Another guard handed him the mail at the door. As he walked back he shouted," Mail call man!"

They stood in a line.They wait to hear their name called. Their name is called.There handed their mail.Then they go back to their bunk. Charles received a few pieces of mail. He went back to his bed and sat down. He received a few letters. One was from Barbara. It read..

Dear Charles,

"I hope this letter finds you in good health. May God be watching over you. I know it's hard in there. It's almost over. So happy we've been writing.

I enjoyed your letters. I remember the time we took a ride to South Carolina from Crossville in that old Chevy truck. You put more miles on me than that old truck! No one needs to know that. Hah!

I enclosed a check for $200.00. That should last you till you get out. You only have three more weeks. If you need more money just text me. I need to go I'll see you when you get out. Take care of yourself. Its only a few weeks.

Sincerely,

Barbara Burns

Charles sat at the edge of his bed. He thought about the two of them. They are crazy bitches.They've hated each other from childhood. They both want me. They put me in the middle of it.

I love both of them. I'm not used to killing. They want to kill each other. I'm going to pretend. I'm not gonna help. When the time comes I will have no part of it.

Barbara was in love with Charles. She was so sad when they broke up. He is a handsome man. He had blonde hair, muscles on his chest and strong arms. Barbara admired his physique.

Barbara arranged a job for him in construction. He will be working on the highway extension. The new road was coming from the east of Franklin. An old friend she was dating hired him. He didn't know him but he took Barbara's word.

She needed to keep him away from Clara. She knew that he loved her. They won't find him at her house. Her Mother would betray her. She would tell Clara that he was there. Sooner or later Clara would wonder where he was. She knew it was his time to be out. She would be looking for him.

She arrived at the bus stop. There was no one around. She still had another 15 minutes. The bus came down the road. She took a few things out of the front seat and move them to the back. There was plenty of room for Charles to sit comfortably.

The bus pulled up to the terminal entrance. Barbara's heart began to beat rapidly. It was 11 years since their last meeting. She couldn't wait to see him. She opened the door, jumped out and ran to the bus

She was quite excited. She seen him come down the stairs and exit the bus. He had two big bags in his hands. She walked up to him. She offered to hold one. He gave her one of the bags. They both walk to the car.

She popped the trunk and they put the bags in. She close the trunk. Charles grabbed her. His rippled muscle arms wrapped around her. He pulled her close to his solid body. She was excited. The strong bulging muscles felt so good against her body. long time since Barbara had a man.

She felt his penis throbbing against her vagina. He hadn't had a female for a long time. She knew that she was going to get seduced. They look at each other and lip locked. Their lips wouldn't come apart. The kisses were juicy and wet.

Clara pushed him away.

"Come on, let's get back to the house. We can continue this there." She said

Charles was thrilled to see her. Clara was in his heart though.

They both got in the car and drove to Barbara's. When they got out of the car. Barbara open the trunk and they took the bags out. They brought them in the house. They were standing by the couch.

Charles grab her again. She resisted this time. She told him. "I know that you're going to go back to my sister. I'm not gonna let myself get into this. You having me and then leaving me. I love you and I don't want to be hurt."

Charles turned to her and said. "You won't get hurt I need you baby. It's been a long time Barbara don't deny me. Let's go in the bedroom baby. I need to feel love and your breasts are beautiful."

He started taking her blouse down. Then he unbuttoned her bra. She pulled them off. Her breast became exposed. He noticed the beautiful thick breasts and the shape of her nipples. They were mouth watering. He put his hands around them. He gives them a gentle squeeze.

She started to moan and groan. He pushed up against her and started to grind her with his penis. She started to hug him. They became closer and closer Holding each other. He pushed away and grabbed her hand. They walked into the master bedroom.

They moved to the bed and she went down on him. She opened his pants. His hard throbbing rod poked out from his underwear. She pulled his underwear down.

She grasped the throbbing boner with her hand. She placed it in her lips. She began to give him oral. He bent down and began rubbing her vagina. They both screamed as they climaxed. The ending was sensational.

Claire was getting concerned she hadn't heard from Charles. She asked her mother to call the prison and ask about him. She was told she couldn't have any contact.

Sandra called the prison and spoke to admissions. She was told that Charles was released a week and a half ago. He registered an address in Crossville as his parole address. The address was Barbara's. Now they know the truth. Charles was at Barbara's house.

Sandra thought to herself. How can I not tell her? The first thing she's going to do is go down to Barbara's. I just can't tell her. She got off the phone and looked at Clara.

She said "he's out." They sat and stared at each other.

She was shocked Charles went there. Sandra told her to relax.

"There was a reason why he had to go there. You were in jail. Don't you remember? Just leave it alone. I don't want you to go to your sisters. There will be nothing but trouble."

She responded."I'm not going there, not yet. But I will show up there."

"No you're not Clara. Leave them alone. In time your sister will tell you or Charles. Somehow or another one of them will come to you. They can't keep this from you. You're a family. So just settle down and wait for it to happen." Sandra told her.

She went into the bedroom and Laid on her bed. She thought of Charles. I know Charles is making love to her. It was sickening her. Barbara did it to her again. Like they were in their teenage years.

"Charles has to choose. She thought. It's me or my sister. I've had enough of this. I'm going to kill that bitch . Maybe him too."

Clara turn over and put her face in the pillow. She began to cry. Charles had gone to Barbara. She couldn't believe he betrayed her. It really upset her and broke her heart.

She cried profusely. Sandra walked in the door and looked at her. She looks so pitiful crying in bed like a two-year-old. Sandra sat down at Her side. She begin stroking her back.

Sandra spoke very softly to her. "Clara let it go. He's not worth it Clara. Why are you putting yourself through this. You know you're facing jail time. You can never have a future with him. Let him go.

Maybe your sister can find happiness in him. I know it's hard to do but you need to let him go. Please turn around and give me a hug. Come and cry on your Mother's shoulder. I'll comfort you. Claire looked at her and said. "Mother, thanks for being here. I love you".

The two of them hugged. Clara felt so much better. She loved how close Mother was to her. She trusted her. She would never get this close with Barbara.

Clara was sitting and started thinking. As soon as my Mother gets relaxed I'm going to Barbara's. I want to catch the two of them together.

Somehow or another I'll get Charles attention.

A Perfect set up with him living in her house. We can murder her there and then get rid of the body. This is only going to work if he hasn't fallen in love. He doesn't have nothing to lose and nothing to gain.

When Barbara has money he has money. So if he has her he has the money already. He has to gain something in order to help me. The only thing I can depend on is he still loves me.

Barber ran down the stairs to the lower level of the house. She looked over on the couch and her mother was fast asleep.

"She will understand why I took the car."

She ran out. She was shocked Charles was staying with Barbara.

"I will find that bastard!"She Said to herself.

 I don't understand how he could go to her. He knew what I had planned. He's gonna be shocked when he sees me. I'm gonna pull up to that house and go right up to the door. She though to her self.

It was a long ride. She pulled up in front of the house. She stopped just before the driveway. Turn the lights off and sat there for a moment. The window was open in the living room. The blinds are pulled to the side. She saw Charles and Barbara sitting together on the couch.

They were watching TV. She watched them for a while. She had to figure out a way to get his attention. She opened the door and got out of the car. She walked up the driveway. She figured she would wait until Barbara got up. She would tap on the window and get Charles attention.

She did exactly that. It only took about 15 minutes. Barbara got off the couch. Now was her chance.She kept down an taped on the window. Charles heard Her. He freaked out when he saw her standing there. She waited for him to come outside. He got all red in the face.

If Barbara caught them he would have no place to live. Barbara went to the bathroom. He heard the door close. He ran to the front door and opened it. There was Clara in the doorway.

"What in the fuck are you doing here. You were in jail I didn't have a way home. I needed a place to stay. Clara! Don't get upset. This is going to work perfectly. I have total control now of Her . We can still do this.

It's going to be easier now. Don't be stupid. I can get her to go anywhere.

I will do it! Go back to your mothers and I'll call you." Charles insisted.

Clara said. "You know you're right. Claire agreed with him.

"Are you sure you're gonna do this with me?" Clara asked.

Yes! Charles replied.

"Clara,I just got through saying it.It's the perfect plan. Can't you see it stupid. Get the fuck out of here!" He slammed the door.

Clara ran down the driveway into the car. She started it and drove off. Barbara was tricked. She came back and joined Charles on the couch.

Clara drove back to her mother. She was so happy to see Charles. She was also excited that he was still going to help her. She figured she would wait and see if he calls. Like he said. Days went by and she didn't hear from him.

She paced the floor waiting for the phone to ring. "Somethings up!" She thought. This mother-fucker hasn't called? I'm really getting pissed.

Sandra walked into the room. She looked at Clara and stated. "Have you heard from your sister? Did Charles call you? You don't seem too upset about them being together. Or did you go there without me knowing? Let it come out now Clara. I need to know the truth. I just spoke with your sister." Sandra told her.

"Mother! Yes, I went there. I spoke to Charles. They were on the couch by the window. I waited till she went to the bathroom and I tapped on the glass. He came out the door and we spoke. He was supposed to call me and he hasn't. I am very fucking pissed at him. They are screwing everyday. I don't know what to do." She said,

"The best thing to do is nothing. Forget about it Clara. leave it alone like I told you in the beginning. Is he worth all this heartache? You have more things to think about then him.

You better think about what you're going to tell his judge.

If you don't your ass is going to be back in jail. No lawyer in the world is going to get you off if you don't have a story. Think about that. Put your ambitions into that.

It's three weeks before court."Sandra told her.

A few weeks went by and Charles called her. It was impossible to get away from Barbara. He didn't want to get caught. She was always on his back and at his side. There was no way he'd have a chance to get to a phone. One day she went to the store and left her cell phone. He picked up the phone and called Clara. Conversation went as follows.

"Clara! This is Charles! I promisedI would call. I'm sorry it took so long. I couldn't get away. Since I saw you I have stolen dynamite from work. I am working as a blast setter on the new extension. Have I got a great idea.

This is the perfect plan. I thought about it and I know exactly what we're gonna do. Next Sunday I want you to come here and I will have Barbara out in the garage. I'll tell her something is wrong with the car. When Barbara comes out to the car I'll keep her there. You drive up and do what you need to do. We will clean up the floor. Then I will stuff her in the trunk.

We'll take it from there. It's all going to work so cool. Then you come back and take over her identity. Wait till you see what I Have planned for her. She was excited her plan was about to happen. She couldn't believe that Charles still loved her. He was

willing to get rid of Barbara for her. She jumped for joy. Sandra happened to see her and questioned her. What are you so happy about? Did you talk to Charles? She demanded an answer?.

"None of your business. Yes I did speak with him. I made arrangements to see him. So I think you should keep out of this. It's none of your business. I need him. I can't use your advice sorry. I'm going to see him next weekend." Clara told her Mother.

Clara was nervous and it was almost Sunday. She was thinking about how she would carry out her plan. She knew Charles would probably hold her or help strangle her. She didn't know what his participation was going to be. So she had to have a plan of her own. She packed a gun in her purse that was in her suitcase. She said I'll just blast her with this.

Then we can get rid of her body. That's the best way.

Sunday has arrived. Claire Rose from the bed. She got dressed and went to the bathroom brushing her teeth. She threw some old clothes into a suitcase. She knew her clothing was going to get blood splatter. She packed the bag in the trunk. And headed out.

She drove off to Barbara's house. The hours almost right. It was 1:45 and Charles had told her to be there at two sharp. She was going to make it right on time. She pulled up to the house and seen the garage door open. She seen Charles and Barbara in the garage.

Charles happen to turn around. He had seen her. Barbara wasn't looking so he waved at her. Clara open the door and grabbed the gun. She ran up the drive. She slowly crept behind the car. He kept her positioned in front of the car.

No one could see what was going on across the street. There were no houses on that side. She only had neighbors on each side. Charles turned Barbara around and hugged her. He began kissing her. She was kept busy an unaware that Claire was in the garage. Clara snuck up very slowly and shot her in the back.

Charles was in shock. He had a sense of vomiting. It didn't phase Clara. She had a smile. He let her go. She fell against the car down to the floor

They stood and looked at each other. Clara was amazed. The plan worked. They had waited 11 years to do this. It was time to clean everything up and get rid of the body. Charles went into the house and carried out a rug.

Charlie spread the rug out on the floor. Charles grabbed Barbara's hands and Clara had her feet. They laid her on the rug. Each of them grabbed an end and started rolling it over her. They carried the body to Clara's car. They put her in the trunk.

They went back in the house and cleaned up. They wash the blood off themselves and changed clothes. She put on Barbara's clothes. She changed her look.

They went in the garage and scrub the floor. The area was cleaned. Charles instructed Clara to walk out of the garage.

He followed her and push the button for the door. The door lowered. They both walked to the car and got inside. They drove off. Charles told her to head down I 40 east.

Claire said."I know where to go."

" That's right babe! To the cave." He responded.

The two of them drove east and I 40 towards Gatlinburg Tennessee. The cave's location was deep within the mountain. They rested at a rest area. Clara went into the store to buy some gum and cigarettes .

Charles got out of the car and went into the men's room. He took his cell phone with him. He dialed Sandra's number. The phone began to ring. It rang several times. Sandra answered.

"Hello." She said.

"Sandra this is Charles! Clara killed Barbara. We're going to Tennessee now to get rid of the body. We should be back in two days. I told you I could get her to do it. What do you want me to do from here?"Charles said.

"Good job Charles. We'll be happy with all the money! We just have to get rid of Clara. When you're on your way back call me. I'm going to call that cop Fuller. I'll tell him that Clara has gone after Barbara. He'll get to the house quickly. The shit will hit the fan!" Sandra told Charles.

"That's cool! We'll figure out the rest when I get back. I gotta go! Clara is probably back in the car. I'll give you a call and we'll go from there.

Thank you! I know you'll figure it out. Bye" Charles tried to hang up the phone.

"Wait! Charles you'll be rich if this works. Don't fuck up!," Barbara told him.

Charles went back to the car. Clara looked at him through the window. He sat in the car and she asked, "What took you so long? We have to go and you know what's in the trunk!"

"Get over it Clara. I had to go to the bathroom. I can't tell my body how long it's to shit. I know you're nervous just relax! Everything's fine Clara. She hasn't started to stink yet. How many more miles is it to that cave? Do you know Charles asked?"

"Probably 2 1/2 hours Charles. If you don't decide to stop again. Put the car in drive and let's get going." Claire was very demanding.

She was starting to really get out of it. The two of them didn't say a word for the balance to the ride. They arrived in front of the cave. Charles got out of the driver's seat.

"Back the car up into the cave and make sure it is inside the opening. "He told Clara.

Clara got into the driver's seat. She did as she was instructed. The car was inside the opening. She turned it off and got out. She went back to the trunk.

They lifted Barbara out of the trunk. They carried her and laid her next to the truckers body. Clara went back to the trunk. She removed the bloody clothes. She picked up the bag and laid it next to Barbara.

Clara, go outside and run down the hill. I'll meet you there. Clara didn't hesitate. She ran down the side of the mountain. She waited for him at the campground.

Charles went back into the trunk of the car. He got six sticks of dynamite that he had taken from work. He sat and inserted the fuse. He lit the wick and ran like a jack rabbit.

He was a considerable distance from the opening. The dynamite exploded. The earth closed the mouth to the cave. The bodies inside were buried never to be unearthed again.

Charles ran down the dirt road and join Clara at the bottom.

"What was that? What did you do?" Clara asked Charles.

I told you I had something planned. I took some dynamite from work. Cops will never find those bodies or that car. Let's go and heist us a car. We can't walk back.

They walked into the campground. They walked around the lanes. They were looking for a car with the keys in the ignition. They spotted one.

The police had begun to arrive. They were curious as to what exploded. People from the campground started running near the explosion. During all the commotion they spotted a car. The police begun to arrive. They were curious what exploded? People heard the explosion. They ran away from the explosion.

Charles used the diversion to his advantage. Charles spotted a fast car. He had to have it. He told Clara to meet him at the exit.

Charles walked around the camper where the car was parked. He quietly open the door and snuck inside. Clara waited down the road. He started the car and drove away from the camper.

He bent over and open the passenger door. Clara jumped in and they sped off. They weren't noticed due to the commotion taking place.

The car was pretty cool. It was quick. A Camaro with a 455 engine and Muncie four speed. It really moved down the road. Charles started racing people on the highway going back.

They passed a few cops on the side of the road. They drove through without incident. There was no trouble all the way to Crossville. The ride back was four hours.

Upon arrival at the house. Charles went inside and called a rental agency. They rented a storage locker. The storage units were a half a block down from the house. Charles walked down to the storage office and rented the unit.

He paid cash for the unit for a month. From the office he called Clara. She drove the car down there. She met him at the storage unit opening. He opened the door and Clara drove the car inside. They both got out. Charles close the door and put a lock on it. The car was never seen again. Clara an Charles returned to the house.

"The mission was successful!" Clara told Charles. Charles didn't make any comment. They opened the door and went back inside. Clara started to cook dinner. Charles went into the bathroom to call Sandra.

"Hello Sandra! We're back! Did you figure out what to do from here?"

"Yes I did! Tomorrow I'm going to call Fuller and get him to go there. When the cops get there you'll run come out. You need to act this out like a professional! Tell them she held you hostage. I'll take care of the rest. I will text you after I place the call. That

way you'll know there on the way."
Sandra told him.

"That sounds great Sandra. I got this.
I know exactly what to do from
here."

He hung up the phone and went back
in the kitchen. Clara looked at
Charles and said,"I am Barbara. How
do you like me?" She asked.

"That's true Clara. You have to take
over her identity. You need to start
dressing like her.

No one will know. I know dear we got
the house! Everything! Thank you so
much for helping me.

Charles looked at her. He knew she
was a nutcase. He didn't want to

upset her. He was petrified of her. He was just waiting until the police got there. He would definitely leave her. He felt so bad . He didn't like what they did to Barbara. That was all planned. Sandra put it together.

To get rid of both of the girls. She said that she would split everything with him. Right to the penny. Then he can go on his way. That's what they had planned. They put this together while he was in prison.

Barbara waited till the next morning. She picked up the phone and called Fuller at the station. She told him that Clara went down by Barbara's house.

He was in the basement. He phoned her."He said that she was threatening him and Barbara. "

Sandra told fuller to get there as fast as he can. Barbara was planning to kill the both of them.

Charles went to Barbara's when he got out of prison. Clara was very upset. He is in the basement on the phone talking to me. She's upstairs and she's nutty. You need to get there. Hurry! Bring backup!" She hung up.

Charles was waiting that morning for a text message. He was downstairs having coffee at the table. Clara was upstairs in the bedroom dressing.

There was an alert on his phone. He looked and it was a text message from Sandra.

" Fuller is on his way. Get ready." She told him.

Charles called Clara to come down stairs. She joined him at the table. He poured her a cup of coffee.

Charles got up and went and unlock the front door. He also opened the garage door. Clara was unaware of his betrayal. She was sitting at a table relaxing. Charles was a nervous wreck. He stayed close to the door. Fuller pulled up in front of the house.

Fuller was walking toward the house. Charles ran back into the kitchen and told Clara the cops were there. Clara had a gun in her pocket. She said" let him in!

Fuller walked in the door and looked. Clara was standing in the room. It was filled with smoke. Satan began to speak.

"Clara you need to kill that cop!" He said,

She watched the officer approach her. Satan kept speaking to her telling her how to proceed. Charles was standing by the wall freaking out.

She watched the officer approach her. Satan kept speaking to her. Pull the trigger. Charles was standing by the wall freaking out.

"Kill him! Satan said. Either that or you're going to get killed. You'll be in jail for the rest of your life. You need to do what I told you. If you have to. Finish off Charles. Take both of them."

Charles ran out the door and Clara started screaming. "Where are you going Charles what are you doing. Don't leave me! You asshole!. Fuller came at her and grabbed her arm. Clara put a bullet right through his head. He fell to the floor. Charles came back into the room and looked at the floor. He was totally shocked that she did that. She put the gun to her head and said to Charles.

"I can't handle this. Satan has told me to kill myself. I love you Charles!"

Charles just stood there. He didn't know what to say. He didn't want to get shot. She pulled the trigger. The bullet went right in her head. He fuck-in couldn't believe what he just witnessed. She was dead.

The gun dropped to the floor. Both bodies laid in a pool of blood. Human flesh and brain matter splattered in the hallway.

Charles ran out of the house. He was cry was frantic. Squads pulled up in front of the house and they grabbed him. He explained to them what was going on inside. He fell to his knees. The police comforted Charles.

Barbara arrived at the house. She grabbed Charles. She took him back to her house.

It was a few weeks after the incident that she paid him off. Charles hugged her and walked out the doorIt's been one year since she last saw Charles. He has never called or written after they split. Charles took off to the east. He had money and the start for a new life. He was done being a bum. He turned into a Saved Christian. His new life had begun.

Sandra began thinking about Charles. She seen him in a different light. She knew Charles could snitch her out. If for some reason he opened his mouth everything would be lost. She set out to find him.

She called his family and asked if they had seen him. No luck. None of his family knew his whereabouts . She went to the post office. She acquired a forwarding address. He relocated to Gatlinburg Tennessee.

She got lucky! It took her a few days to figure out what to do. She thought, he will always be in danger.

On the other hand she could find him and handle the problem.

She wasn't too sure how to move forward. This was upsetting her for several months. She couldn't get him off her mind. Sandra was becoming paranoid and troubled. The paranoia was driving her nuts. She had become schizophrenic.She was having horrible thoughts.

Sandra tried everything to get Charles off her mind. But the demons haunted her. She started having visions of Satan. The episodes were troubling. She didn't know how to handle it. They frightened her. Her visits to the doctor and the psychiatrist were hopeless. Satan became a normal stage in her thoughts. She was being told to eliminate him. She couldn't do it. It wasn't in her.

Charles was working at one of the museums. She drove to Gatlinburg. She rented a room on the strip. It took her two weeks to locate him.

She watched every move he made. She knew what kind of car he was driving. He found a girlfriend that he was staying with. She had to come up with a plan. She had to get rid of both of them.

Sandra just couldn't get herself to go forward with this. She resisted the commands of murder from Satin. She didn't have the willpower to hold him off. It was becoming overwhelming! Satan demanded she kill them.

Sandra couldn't handle the pressure from Satan. She was frightened to stay in the room. She thought a drive would do her good. She grabbed a sweater and went out to the car. She got in and drove away.

She drove south out of town. The mountains had curvy roads, and drop-offs at the roadside. She was approaching a lookout at the top of a curve. She pulled into the lookout. There were a few tourists standing.

They looked over the mountainside. The beauty was breathtaking. The treetops stood tall above the smoke. It swallowed the view of the distant mountains. The sun was going down. There was an orange glow behind the trees in the distance. The sun went down and the tourists departed.

Sandra was standing alone at the overlook. She was accompanied by Satan. She decided to take a walk. Satan told her to cross the raging river. She was instructed to cross to the other side of the waterfalls.

She noticed some fallen trees crossing the water. It was the way to cross. She jumped over the rail and walked towards the waterfall. There was a deep drop over the side into the gorge. The water fell rapidly over the mountain side. She grabbed a stick to keep her balance. She walked on the logs going across the river. With the waterfall raging beneath her feet.

Satan pushed her. Her balance was lost and over the waterfall she went. She tumbled down to the bottom of the gorge.

Her body floated down the river. It disappeared. She wasn't seen again. Did she survive?

It was about three hours later. A policeman happened to stop at the Overlook. He noticed her car sitting there. Know one was standing by the rail. He exited his car and went to investigate. The door was unlocked. The keys were in the ignition. He stood firm and turned. He walked in all directions looking for someone.

There wasn't anyone to be found. Sandra's purse was sitting on the seat. He opened the door and reached for it. He pulled out an identification card. The lady was from Crossville.

He went back to his cruiser. He called her name into dispatch at the station. The dispatcher checked her license number. They received information on Sandra. They knew who she was. The car was towed to the pound. *It* took several weeks for the police to connect him.

This officer was investigating Evelyn's disappearance case. He worked with Fuller on the investigation. He put out an alert for Charles. His whereabouts were unknown. Tolin received a tip. Charles was in Gatlinburg. He hit the streets to find him.

He drove up and down the main streets. He spent hours talking to people. He carried a mug shot from the Indiana State prison. He showed it to many people down the strip.

No one recognized him. He went into a donut shop for coffee. He asked the waitress if she knew Charles. He pulled out the picture and showed it to her.

She said yes! "That guy just started working at the museum across the street."

Tolin got the first break in the case! He walked across the street and went into the museum. He went up to the counter.

He asked the attendant," Is there a Charles working here?"

He showed him the picture of Charles. The attendant identified Charles. "Yes! I'll get him for you." He said."

He walked into the back and Charles came out. He introduced himself.

Tolin questioned Charles. He didn't have any information about Sandra's disappearance.

He asked Charles how long he's been in Gatlinburg. Charles was shocked that Sandra's name was brought up. He hadn't seen her. He told Tolin it was about a year or so. The officer did not agree with his answers. He cuffed Charles and took him into custody. Charles was booked on a charge of murder.

The police believe Charles went to the mountain side with her. He pushed her into the river. There was some foul play. They said he argued with her. Charles was accused of murder. They asked him about the remains of the trucker and Evelyn.

The bodies of the trucker and Evelyn were never found. The car in storage was found three months after Clara's death.

Charles was in jail for eight months. He was acquitted of Sandras murder. He walked out of the Gatlinburg courthouse. The state bought him a ticket to Indianapolis and he left town.

Charles found a one room flat in Indianapolis. He rented it. He went back to work for the cement project on the highway. He worked there for about seven months and quit.

Charles was a troubled individual. He refused to make any friends. Clara was the love of his life. He was miserable. Charles drove back to Tennessee. He took a ride up into the mountains. He went to the place Sandra fell over the falls.

Charles stopped the car at the Overlook. Opened the door and left the car. He walked over to the gorge and looked out. He raised his hand and threw the keys down the side of the ridge. He was headed south to the road.

Charles was discouraged and felt very lonely. He wasn't sure where he was headed. He had to leave Tennessee. Charles stood out on the road. He turned facing the oncoming traffic. He stuck his thumb out and started walking backwards down the road. He didn't care who picked him up as long as he could get out of Tennessee.

A few cars passed and ignored him. He had walked about half a mile before someone stopped. A car pulled ahead of him. It pulled over towards the shoulder.

The person rolled down the window and said,"Come on hop in!"

He looked inside the car and saw Sandra. The image inside the car was Satan. He was in Sandra's body. He's going to make Charles believe it's her. He entered the car.

He said to her,"I thought you were dead.

Satan replied,"I survived the fall."I Didn't expect to pick you up on the road! I was going to West Virginia.

Charles looked at her and disbelief. He touched her to make sure she was real. Charles was convinced that it was really Sandra. Satan had him fooled. They sped off down the road towards Virginia.

As they were driving they started having a conversation.

Charles said,"I can't believe! How did you survive? Everyone thought you were dead. You went over the river fall. The dive had to be 400 to 500 feet. I'm surprised your body didn't get torn apart. That should have happened as you hit the bottom. I'm surprised the undercurrent hadn't drown you. Do you recall anything?"

Satan was laughing inside as Charles questioned him. He knew that he had Charles. Satan had a big surprise for Charles. Satan kept driving. They kept driving while having conversation. They made a few stops for snacks and beers.

"I really don't recall all the details. I know I hit the bottom of the waterfall hard. It knocked me out. I found myself floating down the river. I turned over and started swimming to the edge. I didn't think I was going to make it. My head was bleeding. I hit the rocks under the water.

I floated a mile or more down the river from the waterfall. I grabbed onto a log. I held on tight. I was floating down the river. The rapids took me along. I finally reached the river edge. I managed to pull myself up out of the water. There was sludge beneath my feet. I was loaded with mud from my head to my toes. I crawled up into the shrubs and layed in the grass. I had to regain my senses.

I stayed there for a while and then Rose. I found an old tub that was laying on the river edge. I filled it with water. I rinsed my body off. I had to pour four tubs over my head. It took most of the mud off of me. I was clean enough to proceed forward and find me a way out of the brush. I'm surprised I survived Charles."

"What did you do from there. The police towed your car. How did you get to Gatlinburg?"Charles asked.

"I thumbed my way back. A man took me back. He asked me why I was full of mud? I told him what happened. I fell in the river. He was very nice. He drove me back to Gatlinburg. When I got back I rented a motel room. I took a shower.

I must've slept 2 1/2 days. When I woke up I was in a twilight. There was blood all over the sheets. I had several cuts and abrasions on my forehead. There were more on the back of my head. I was so tired I didn't notice them. I got up and took care of the wounds.

I had to cut some of my hair off . I shared my head down to the wounds. I was hurting. Plenty of cuts on my legs and arms. I stayed in that room for about three weeks.I was fully healed beforeI went out. I was never cut that bad in my life Charles. I thought I was going to die. I was living on aspirins. I had sandwiches from the restaurant. I smoked three packs of cigarettes.

Once I felt better I called the car rental agency. They brought me over a nice compact. " Satan explained.

"Does anybody know you're alive?" Charles asked.

"I don't think so. I didn't tell anybody. I surely didn't call the police! Why?" She asked

"I just got out of jail because of you. I was acquitted for your murder. Cops thought You were pushed over the fall. I sat in County for seven months.

Once I got out I caught a bus to Indianapolis . I rented a one room flat. It was in someone's old man's house. I went to work on the road crew. They had me cutting concrete.

I stayed up there for almost a year. I decided I didn't want to do that. I needed to get away. So many people were talking to me about my crimes. I can't stand it. I was so embarrassed at times I wanted to hide. More than once I stayed in my room instead of going to work. Everybody knew I was in the penitentiary. I had to get out of there.

I made up my mind and called my job. I told the supervisor I quit. He couldn't believe that I was going to walk out of them. I didn't care. I was tired of being humiliated. I packed my bags and put them in the car. I went downstairs and I knocked on my landlord's door.

When he answered I simply told him I am packed and I'm leaving. He looked at me in shock and I handed him the key. I didn't just turn down the walk to the car.

I opened the door, got in, and drove off. That was the last I saw of Indy. That was yesterday. It took me four hours to drive down here. I wanted to see where you were killed. I guess everyone got fooled. I sit in jail. Well! well! Here we are Sandra?" He said.

Satan answered by saying,

"I'm really sorry Charles. I didn't do this on purpose. I know it was hard for you to do time. One thing came out of it. You were acquitted. Be thankful for that.

Now we found each other and we could be together. I've have a lot of money from the estate. So let's just enjoy this time and enjoy our lives. What do you think? I know your carrying a bank roll!" Satin Replied.

Unfortunately you're wrong Sandra. Most of that money I spent on the lawyer for my trial. I've been living off of it. Plus all the commissary in the penitentiary. There's $6000 left. But I know you got a pocket full." Charles replied.

Satan started to laugh inside. If Charles only knew what he did have. He has a million dollars if he wanted. Charles was fooled and tricked. He fell right into Satan's spell.

They drove 150 miles south towards Virginia. Charles was becoming quite tired. Satan was watching Charles as he closed his eyes and fell asleep. He knew that he didn't have to go to West Virginia. He just told Charles some bullshit. So he pulled over to the road. He let Charles take a nap.

When Charles rose he looked around out the window.

"We did not travel too far!" Charles asked?

Satan replied, "I pulled over and joined you napping. We're gonna be moving now it's getting dark. There is a sever curve in the road ahead in the mountains."

I'm not worried about it. You seem like you know how to handle the car. Just slow down if they become too severe. I'll be your second set of eyes. They drove through the mountains for a while and Satan looked over at Charles.

"Charles! Was Clara seeing Satan and having spells? Did she ever say anything to you about this?" Satan asked.

"She was alway seeing Satan. He would tell her to do things. She described how she murdered people. She did some awful things. Most of that came from her smoking crack. I guess the demons went to her head. That's all she ever talked about was Satan smoking her.

I never really believed her. I thought it was a joke or hallucination. You gotta be nuts to think that stuff is true. I became a reborn Christian. I don't believe in that. I didn't think Satan would ever bother me. Why do you ask?" Charles inquired?

Satan looked over at Charles replying. "Charles I got news for you. I am Satan! I came here in Sandra's body to get you."Satan told Charles.

Suddenly the doors locked. Satan let go of the wheel. The car was driving on its own. Charles was freaking out. Satan looked at him and told him,

"I'm gonna kill you! Do you see that Cliff? That's the cliff to hell.Charles I got rid of Claire and Sandra and now it's your turn. You can jump! I sealed the doors! They can't open. You are a murderer and your God isn't forgiving you for that. Your ass is going with me to the pit of fire!" Satin said.

The accelerator pedal started hitting the floor. This speed was excessively fast. The speedometer hit 100. The car was swaying around the curves. Charles didn't know what to do. He tried the brakes and the pedal hit the floor. The road came to an end. Satan directed the car to go straight over the cliff

When they reached the cliff the car went air bound. Down the mountain side it went. Smashing into the boulders and bricks. The car knocked trees down at the bottom of the gorge. It burst into flames. As the smoke cleared Satan rose from the roof of the car. He came through the roof in a puff of smoke. Charles was never found! Charles was thrown into the brush.

MURDER: IN
Franklin County

WRITTEN BY:
JOHN SYLVESTER